AN EDWARD THE UNREADY BOOK

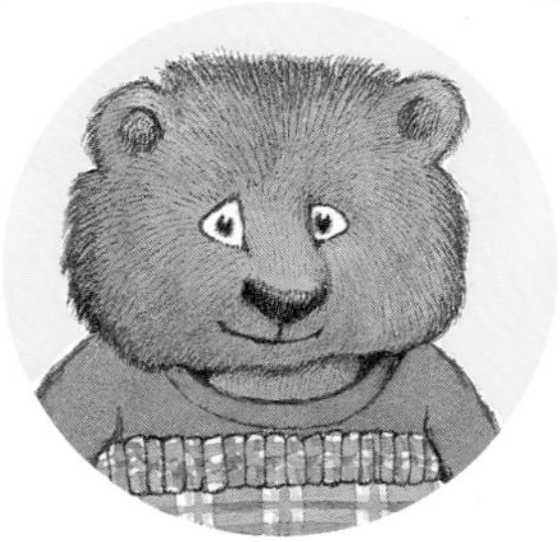

EDWARD
UNREADY FOR SCHOOL

· ROSEMARY WELLS ·

Dial Books for Young Readers *New York*

for Phyllis

Monday was the first day of play school.
"Are you ready, Edward?" asked Edward's father.

But Edward was not ready.
So his father had to dress him.

Edward's mother fed him his Cream of Wheat.

Together they put him in the car.

But Edward had to go back for Bunny.

"I'll hide," he said, "and they'll never find me."

But they did.

Back went Edward into the car.
His seat belt was securely fastened.

"Now we are ready at last!"
said Edward's mother.

At school Edward's teacher was all smiles.

Everyone was happy and busy.

But Edward didn't want to be happy and busy.

He wanted to go home.

All week long everyone tried to make Edward happy.

But Edward couldn't get happy.

By mistake, he hid in the wrong bathroom.

"NO!" said the girls.

Friday Edward's teacher said, "Not everyone is ready for the same things at the same time."

"Well, we'll just take him home until he *is* ready,"
said Edward's mother and father.

"Be ready soon!" shouted everybody.
"I'm ready right now," said Edward.

"What are you ready for?" asked Edward's father.
"I'm ready for my sandwich," said Edward.

"And Bunny is ready for his bug soup."

Published by Dial Books for Young Readers
A Division of Penguin Books USA Inc.
375 Hudson Street
New York, New York 10014

Copyright © 1995 by Rosemary Wells
All rights reserved
Printed in the U.S.A.
First Edition
1 3 5 7 9 10 8 6 4 2

Library of Congress Cataloging in Publication Data
Wells, Rosemary.
Edward unready for school / Rosemary Wells.
p.   cm.—(Edward the unready)
Summary: Edward, a shy young bear unready
for play school, feels out of place surrounded by students
who are ready, busy, and happy.
ISBN 0-8037-1884-5
[1. Bears—Fiction. 2. Play schools—Fiction. 3. Schools—Fiction.]
I. Title. II. Series: Wells, Rosemary. Edward the unready.
PZ7.W46843Ecj   1995   [E]—dc20   95-7890   CIP   AC

The artwork for each picture
is an ink drawing with watercolor painting.